DORRIE
and the Witch's Imp

by Patricia Coombs

Lothrop, Lee & Shepard Company
New York

Other books by Patricia Coombs

Dorrie and the Amazing Magic Elixir
Dorrie and the Birthday Eggs
Dorrie and the Blue Witch
Dorrie and the Fortune Teller
Dorrie and the Goblin
Dorrie and the Haunted House
Dorrie and the Weather-Box
Dorrie and the Witch Doctor
Dorrie and the Wizard's Spell
Lisa and the Grompet
Molly Mullett
Mouse Café

3 4 5
Library of Congress Cataloging in Publication Data
Coombs, Patricia.
  Dorrie and the witch's imp.
  SUMMARY: The wicked Gloris conjures up a double for Dorrie, but the double arouses suspicion with its unnatural neatness and courtesy.
  [1. Witches—Fiction] I. Title.
PZ7.C7813Dr   [Fic]   75-5504
ISBN 0-688-41704-3   ISBN 0-688-51704-8 lib. bdg.

for Anne Wendy Brennan

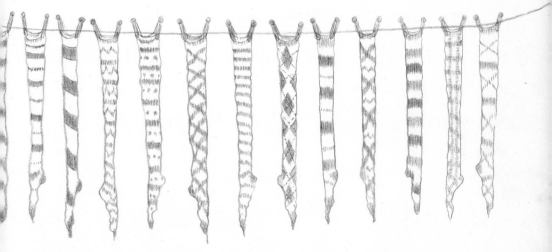

This is Dorrie. She is a witch. A little witch. Her hat is on crooked and her socks never match. Her house is tall and dark and spooky. She lives there with her black cat Gink and her mother the Big Witch and Cook.

One day Dorrie and Gink went downstairs. The Big Witch ran by with the duster. Cook ran by with the laundry.

Dorrie and Gink followed the Big Witch into the parlor. "Mother," said Dorrie, "why are you rushing around so fast?"

"There's trouble in Glumglen. And it's getting worse," said the Big Witch. "Ever since those nice witches moved there, awful things have been happening to them. Mud comes out of the faucets. Windows crack. Knots are tied in their clothes. Creaks and skreeks and pinches keep them awake at night. Notes were stuck all around saying: BEWARE THE BIG WITCH! GET OUT FAST!"

"Oh, my," said Dorrie. "They think you're to blame!"

The Big Witch nodded. "They are very angry and ready to fight Witchville. They agreed to come here for dinner tonight to talk about it. It's our last chance to convince them that we're not to blame. And to find out who *is* trying to drive them out of Glumglen. Nothing must go wrong at the dinner party tonight!"

The Big Witch dusted the piano so hard that feathers flew out of the duster. Dorrie sneezed. So did Gink.

"Let me dust for you, Mother," said Dorrie.

"Thank you. I'm so nervous!" The Big Witch looked at the clock. "Oh! I have to fly into town and get my new dress for the dinner tonight!" The Big Witch rushed off to get her cloak and broomstick.

There was a knock at the back door.

"Oh, bother!" cried the Big Witch. "Cook must have locked herself out." She ran to the door and opened it. It wasn't Cook. An old witch dressed in gray was standing there.

"My name is Gloris," said the witch. "Cook's sister is very sick and needs her. Cook had to leave in a big hurry. She sent me to take her place."

"Oh, no!" cried the Big Witch, turning pale. "The dinner tonight has to go *just right*. Nothing must go wrong. It's very important!"

"Don't worry. Run along. I'll take care of *everything*. I'm a very good cook. Ah, and I do like children!" said Gloris, as Dorrie came into the kitchen. "The dear child can show me where things are."

The Big Witch looked at Gloris. She looked at Dorrie. She looked at the clock. "Well," said the Big Witch, "if Cook sent you, it must be all right. Now I must fly!"

The Big Witch got on her broomstick and flew away over the treetops. Dorrie waved goodbye.

Gloris rubbed her hands and smiled and peered around the kitchen.

"I'll help," said Dorrie.

"That will be nice, dearie," said Gloris.

"The name is DORRIE," said Dorrie.

"That's nice, dearie. I'll make the soup first," said Gloris.

Dorrie got out the soup kettle. Gloris put water in it and put it on the stove. Dorrie got out the carrots. Gloris began throwing them in.

"You didn't scrape the carrots!" said Dorrie. "Mother won't eat soup if the carrots aren't scraped and washed. Here, like this." Dorrie began to scrape carrots and wash them. She turned the faucet too hard. Water splashed all over Gloris.

Gloris yelled and scowled, "GET OUT! GET OUT . . . uh, the onions, will you, dearie? There's a dear child."

Dorrie got out a sack of onions. The string broke. Onions rolled all over the floor. Gloris stumbled and slipped and shrieked. She started to yell at Dorrie again and stopped. "I'll finish the soup, dearie. Go dust something."

Dorrie and Gink went into the dining room. Dorrie left the door open a crack. "Gink," whispered Dorrie, "that witch is up to something. She can't cook. Look at that. She just tossed the onions in without peeling them! And she likes children the way I like castor-oil."

As Dorrie watched, Gloris began taking some little bunches of stuff from her sleeves. She dumped them into the soup and stirred.

"There," mumbled Gloris, "Wither-Wort, Viper-Vetch, and Fly-By-Night. A few swallows of soup, and Glumglen will be mine! But I mustn't lose my temper or I'll never get this soup into those bothersome witches. I have to get some help. That kid is driving me crazy."

"Gink," whispered Dorrie, "those weeds are used for really BAD spells. And the only place they grow is in Glumglen! We've got to watch Gloris very carefully until Mother gets back."

Dorrie skipped into the kitchen with Gink. Gloris was putting celery and tomatoes into the soup.

"You didn't peel the tomatoes! You didn't chop up the celery! When mother sees that mess she'll throw it out," said Dorrie.

"OH, SHUT . . . UH . . . shut the door, dearie," said Gloris, scowling and fishing the tomatoes and celery out of the soup.

"I'll help," said Dorrie. She skidded on an onion and bumped into Gloris. Gloris screeched and dropped the hot tomatoes on the floor.

"I'm sorry," said Dorrie. "I'll clean it up."

"Do that, dearie. There's a good child. I have to go to the bathroom." Gloris started down the hall.

"Wait! You don't know where it is," said Dorrie, running after her.

"I'll find it! I'll find it!" yelled Gloris. She whizzed into Cook's bathroom and slammed the door and locked it. "I'll be out in a minute. Go back and clean up the floor, dearie."

"Come on, Gink," said Dorrie, loudly. She stomped back toward the kitchen. Then she spun around and tiptoed back to the bathroom door. She looked through the keyhole.

There was Gloris, mixing up some kind of brew in Cook's washbowl and stirring it with Cook's toothbrush. She took a Magic Stick from her sleeve and waved it over the black, swirly clouds coming out of the washbowl.

NATTER, NATTER, UGLY IMP,
WICKED ONE, COME QUICK AS QUICK!
AS DORRIE'S LOOK-ALIKE, YOU'LL TRICK
HER MOTHER INTO THINKING YOU
ARE DORRIE AND THAT DORRIE'S YOU
TILL SHE AND THE OTHERS DRINK MY BREW

"Oh, oh," whispered Dorrie. "We're in big trouble! That Imp DOES look like me! Come on, Gink!"

Down the hall they ran. It was too late. In a flash Gloris and Natter had grabbed her.

"Take care of her, Natter. And be quick! We've got work to do. Nothing must go wrong tonight!"

Natter dragged Dorrie down the hall. Dorrie yelled and gave Natter a kick in the shins. Natter squealed and let go. Dorrie raced into the parlor. She jumped behind the couch. Natter jumped after her. Dorrie bit Natter's hand. Over the couch, into the hall went Dorrie. She made a dash for the front door. Natter grabbed her by the ankles. Over and over they tumbled, kicking and biting and pinching.

Gloris came running from the kitchen. "I told you to take care of her, you wretched Imp!" screeched Gloris. She took out her Magic Stick and whacked Dorrie three times, saying:

NO SOUND YOU'LL MAKE,
NO YELL, NO SCREECH
OR EVEN ANY THUMP OR KICK.
THIS SPELL OF SILENCE NONE CAN BREAK
BUT GLORIS WITH HER MAGIC STICK!

With that, Gloris grabbed Dorrie by the feet and Natter took her arms. Down the hall to Cook's bathroom they went. They tossed Dorrie inside with Gink. They slammed the door and locked it.

Back to the kitchen went Natter and Gloris. Quick as a wink they had the soup bubbling. Natter polished and waxed everything in the dining room and set the table perfectly.

"It's going to be a lovely dinner party," grinned Natter.

"Isn't it though!" chuckled Gloris. She rubbed her hands together. "And just to be sure nothing goes wrong, run find the Big Witch's magic and get rid of it. And here, rub this sprig of Wither-Wort on her crystal ball. I don't think she'll suspect anything, but we must be careful!"

Up, up, up the stairs went Natter. Up to the Big Witch's secret room at the top of the tower. Around and around and around went Natter, dumping out all the bottles and boxes and jars of magic. Natter was rubbing the Wither-Wort over the crystal ball when a shadow flashed past the window. The Big Witch was home.

Down, down, down the stairs trotted Natter. The Big Witch was looking all around and smiling.

"Thank you, Gloris. Thank you, Dorrie. You have worked very hard. Everything looks perfect! It's going to be a lovely dinner party!"

"Mother, dear," said Natter, "do let me put your broomstick and cloak away for you."

"What? Oh, yes, all right," said the Big Witch. "I must hurry. It's getting very late."

The Big Witch started up the stairs. She stopped. She frowned. "'Mother, DEAR'?" She looked at Natter trotting into the kitchen. "The socks, the socks match! The hat, the hat is straight! Something is funny here. I'm going to take a look in my crystal ball!" Up, up, up the stairs ran the Big Witch. She flung open the door to her secret room.

"What a mess! My magic, all my magic, gone!" cried the Big Witch. She took out her crystal ball and stared into it, muttering:

CRYSTAL BALL, SHOW ME ALL!
DORRIE'S MISSING, ALL'S NOT RIGHT,
THIS IMPOSTER'S TOO POLITE!

The crystal ball stayed dark and empty. The Big Witch shook it. Nothing happened.

"Oh, drat!" cried the Big Witch. "Something is wrong but I don't know what. Maybe Dorrie got into my magic and changed herself all around."

Downstairs the clock struck six. The swish of broomsticks went past the tower. The Big Witch ran down to her room. She put on her new dress.

She straightened her hat and put on some perfume. She hurried downstairs.

Dorrie and Gink sat in the dark bathroom, listening. Dorrie could hear Gloris and Natter snickering together in the kitchen. She heard the Glumglen witches land in the yard. She could hear everything but she couldn't make a sound herself.

"I've got to *do* something," thought Dorrie. "I've got to keep mother and the Glumglen witches from eating that soup."

She tried to pound on the door. Then she tried to kick it. She couldn't do either one. She was under Gloris' spell.

Then Dorrie heard another sound. Water dripping from a faucet. It gave her an idea. She put the plug in the tub. She turned the water on, hard. She found Cook's bubble bath and poured it all into the tub.

The Glumglen witches knocked at the door. The Big Witch ran to open it.

"Welcome, witches of Glumglen! I'm so glad you came. Dinner is ready and we can talk."

The Glumglen witches clustered together and frowned and looked around. One of them sniffed the air. "Is that MAGIC I smell?"

"Oh, no, no!" said the Big Witch. "That's my perfume you smell. Or else the soup. Here, let me take your cloaks. You can leave your broomsticks in the hall."

"NO!" snapped the Glumglen witches. "We may have to leave SUDDENLY!"

The Big Witch led them into the dining room. They all sat down. They looked under the table. They looked under the napkins. They sniffed the water glasses.

The Big Witch rang a bell. Gloris and Natter came in with the soup and the bowls. Gloris dished up the soup. Natter put a bowl in front of each witch. As Natter put down the last bowl, the Big Witch said:

"Dorrie, it's your bedtime. You've had a busy day.

I could tell by the way my secret room looked. Go to bed. Right now. I'll talk to you later."

"Goodnight. It was nice meeting you," said Natter, with a smile and a curtsey. "Goodnight, Mother dear." Natter trotted out of the dining room and up the stairs to bed.

The Big Witch picked up her spoon. "No Gink! Something is . . ." The Big Witch stopped and stared. So did the Glumglen witches. Bubbles were floating into the dining room, faster and faster, thicker and thicker.

"What a nice idea!" said one witch.

"They taste terrible!" said another witch.

"Excuse me a moment," said the Big Witch. She got up and looked into the hall. Water was flowing across the floor. Bubbles were rising in clouds. The Big Witch started for the bathroom. Gloris came running after her.

"Wait! Wait!" screeched Gloris. "I'll get it! I'll get it! Go eat the soup! You'll spoil the dinner party!"

The Big Witch went back and sat down. "We have a new cook today. She left the water running for a bath." The Big Witch picked up her spoon.

The Glumglen witches stared at the Big Witch and nudged each other. One of them said, "Running a bath in the middle of dinner? She was right here!"

The Big Witch dropped her spoon again. "Of course! So was Dorrie, or whoever that was! I'll be right back!"

"NO!" shouted the Glumglen witches. "This looks like a trap! If you leave this room, we're going, and you'll be sorry!"

The Big Witch looked around the table at the angry faces. "Well, let's get on with dinner then."

With that they all picked up their spoons and began blowing away the bubbles.

Gloris stamped angrily down the hall to the bathroom. Dorrie turned out the light and waited behind the door. The minute Gloris opened it and reached for the light, Dorrie threw herself against the door. It slammed into Gloris, knocking her head over heels into the tub.

Out of the bathroom, down the hall raced Dorrie
and Gink. They jumped up on the table and slid to
the end. The soup bowls sailed into the air and
splashed everywhere.

The Glumglen witches leaped to their feet and grabbed the Big Witch. "Bubbles, floods, smells and spells! Now we know you're the one causing all the trouble! To the cauldrons! To the cauldrons! Bring the prisoner!"

At that moment Gloris came running into the room. When she saw the spilled soup, her face turned bright purple. She took out her Magic Stick and went after Dorrie. Around and around the table they went. Dorrie slid in some soup and fell down. Gloris began screeching and whacking her with the Stick. With the first whack, the spell of silence was broken.

Dorrie let out a yell and Gloris made a dash for the door. "Get that witch! She's the one, not my mother! She put something in the soup!"

The Glumglen witches caught Gloris. They knocked her down and three of them sat on her.

"Mother, dear," said a voice, "your dinner party is very noisy. You woke me . . . oh, oh!" Natter spun around and started upstairs.

Dorrie raced after him and made a grab. She got hold of the dress and it ripped. Out of the dress and down the stairs went Natter.

"Get him! Get that Imp, quick!" cried Dorrie.

The moment the Glumglen witches touched Natter, he vanished like a blot of ink, right through the floor.

The Big Witch took the Magic Stick away from
Gloris and began whacking her with it:

THE SPELL YOU COOKED UP
IN THAT BREW
WHEN I COUNT THREE WILL
FALL ON YOU!

There was a loud PSSSST! Gloris whizzed out
of the room, out the door, and straight up. Up, up,
up she whizzed.

The Big Witch counted to two.

Gloris stopped in midair. Her arms began flap-
ping up and down. She cawed and flew away.

The witches all stared and gasped. "She's turned
into a crow. If we'd eaten the soup, we'd be a flock
of crows!"

The Magic Stick fizzled and turned to ashes in the Big Witch's hand. She smiled.

"I don't think you'll have any more trouble in Glumglen."

Dorrie tugged at the Big Witch's sleeve. "You sent Gloris away too fast. We don't know what she did with Cook."

"All my magic is gone, and that Imp made a mess of my crystal ball!" said the Big Witch.

"Let's look for her out back," said Dorrie. "She was out there with the laundry when Gloris came."

They ran into the backyard and looked all around. They looked under bushes and in the trees. Then Dorrie heard a familiar sound. She pulled the laundry out of the basket. There was Cook, snoring.

Gink rubbed against the basket. Then he licked Cook's nose. Slowly, Cook opened her eyes. "A prince you're not," yawned Cook, "but I'm glad to see you anyway."

They all laughed and went inside. They worked together cleaning up the dining room and mopping up the bathroom and the hall. Cook cooked up a big new dinner.

After dinner they all went into the parlor. The Big Witch played the piano. The Glumglen witches taught them some new songs and they all sang together. Then they played hide-and-seek all over the house.

As the moon went down, the Glumglen witches got on their broomsticks. "Bring everyone in Witchville to Glumglen next Friday," they said. "We'll have a picnic in Glumglen Glade."

Everyone waved goodbye. Dorrie and Gink and the Big Witch and Cook got ready for bed.

"Goodnight, Dorrie," said the Big Witch.

"Goodnight, Mother. Goodnight, Gink dear," yawned Dorrie. And they all fell asleep.